For Ulysses

First published in the United States of America in 2005 by Walker Publishing Company, Inc.
Distributed to the trade by Holtzbrinck Publishers

For information about permission to reproduce selections from this book, write to Permissions, Walker & Company, 104 Fifth Avenue, New York, New York 10011.

Library of Congress Cataloging-in-Publication Data

Hale, Nathan, 1976–
The devil you know / Nathan Hale.
p. cm.
Summary: The Fell family gets frustrated with their house devil so they trade him, but when Ms. Phisto arrives they must try desperately to find the "simple contract" they signed.
ISBN 0-8027-8981-1 (HC) — ISBN 0-8027-8983-8 (RE)
[1. Folklore. 2. Magic. 3. Devil—Folklore. 4. Humorous stories.]

PZ8.1.H137De 2005
[398.2]—dc22
[E]

2004061202

ISBN-13 978-0-8027-8981-5 (HC)
ISBN-13 978-0-8027-8983-9 (RE)

The artist used Golden acrylics on watercolor paper to create the illustrations for this book.

Book design by Nicole Gastonguay

Visit Walker & Company's Web site at www.walkeryoungreaders.com

Printed in Hong Kong

10 9 8 7 6 5 4 3 2 1

Nathan Hale

Walker & Company New York

The Fell family had a devil (a little one).
He came with the house.

He was nothing but trouble.

He was naughty all night . . .

and wicked all day.

He terrified the goldfish . . .

and made the cat go crazy.

HE DID

OF BAD,

ALL KINDS

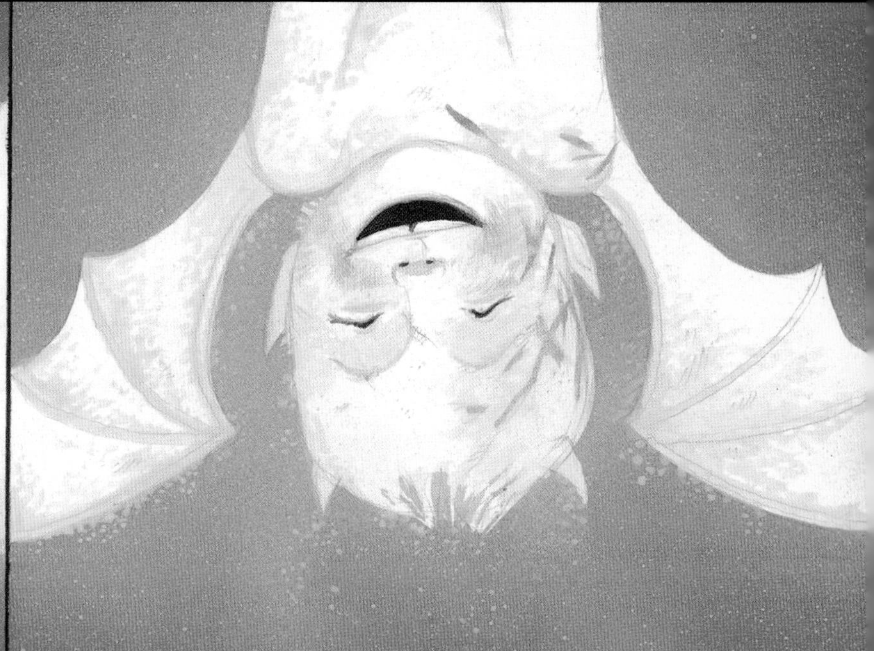

BAD THINGS!

One day, a green lady knocked on the door.

"I hear you have a little devil problem," she said. "I can help you with that. Here is my card. Just burn it if you need me."

Three days later the little devil was extra naughty.

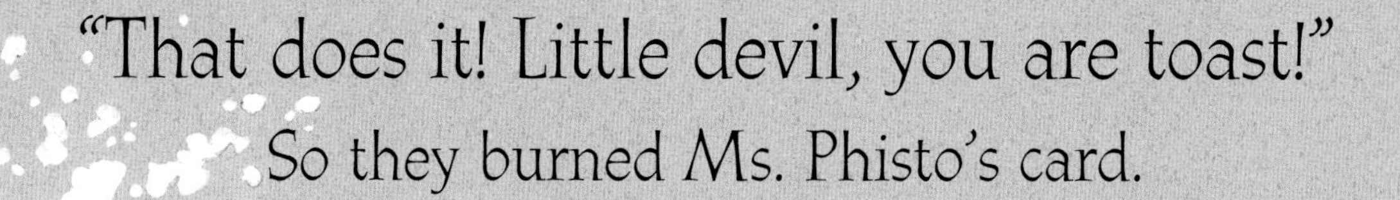

"That does it! Little devil, you are toast!"
So they burned Ms. Phisto's card.

And *POOF!* She appeared.
"So, you want to get rid of your little devil? Well, have a look at this contract," she said.
CONTRACT
WE THE FELL FAMILY DO
SWAP
THEREFORE
PERMANENT
SEALED
FINAL
SIGNED
"The contract says that you will trade your pesky little devil for me. He goes, and I stay. I help out around the house. Very simple. Sound good? Excellent! Sign here, and here and here. Now, I will need some special ingredients to cast a spell."

"Shoe full of salt! Sock full of cocoa!

Send this devil to Acapulco!"

And *POOF!* He disappeared.

"Well," said Ms. Phisto,
"now that's finished.
Will you help me
with my things?"

The Fells carried boxes all day

and half the night.

"Thank you!" said Ms. Phisto. She snapped her fingers and out of the boxes popped a hundred grinning devils.

"I've brought a few helpers," said Ms. Phisto.
"First we'll take care of the dishes.
Then the laundry.
Then the furniture."

"What are you doing to our house!?"

shouted the Fells.

"Well, right here in our contract, it says I have to keep the house neat—that's a lot easier to do without all this stuff.

Everything will go much smoother if you wait outside."

The Fells spent all night outside.

In the morning, Ms. Phisto let them back in.

"Come and see what we've done to the house."

"We've put a lake of fire and brimstone in the kitchen."

"I've put the little devils in the boy's room.

And the big devils in the girls' room."

"And, finally, in the living room—our masterpiece!"

COUCH
HOT SEAT
ADVOCATE
TICKETS

“Please change our house back!” the Fells begged.

“No more! No more!” the Fells pleaded.

They even tried some spells.
“Shoe full of toast!
Hat full of shells!
Send Ms. Phisto
somewhere else!”

But nothing worked.

“Contract,
contract,
contract!”
said Ms. Phisto.

The Fells searched high and low until they found the contract.

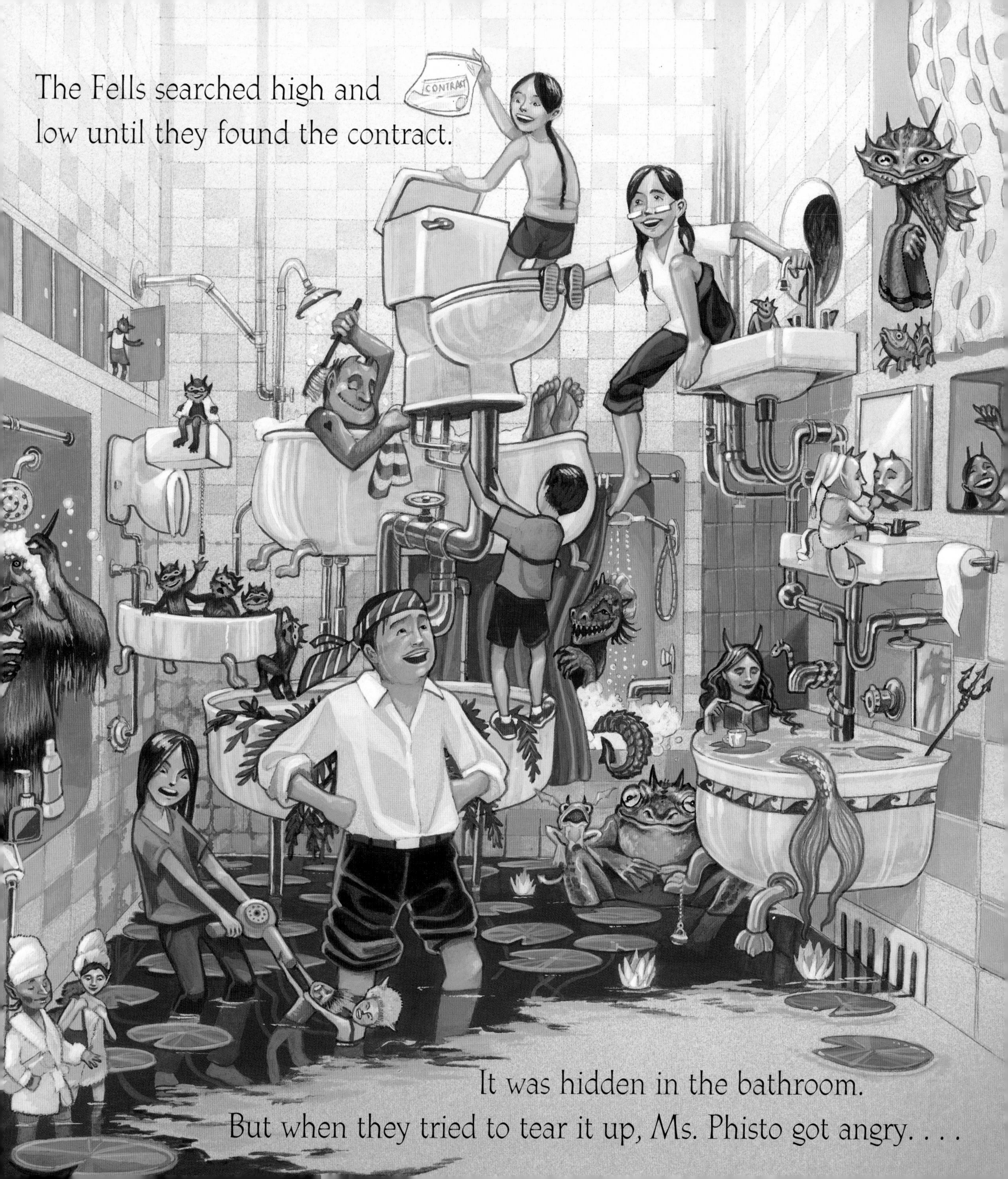

It was hidden in the bathroom. But when they tried to tear it up, Ms. Phisto got angry. . . .

"You people signed a CONTRACT! Don't you know what that means?" boomed Ms. Phisto.

"Sorry," said Ms. Phisto. "I hate to lose my temper like that, but a deal's a deal. You really can't complain."

When you trade the devil you know for the devil you don't, you just might get burned.

The Fells found the special ingredients for one last spell. "Ms. Phisto," they asked, "could you do us a favor?"

"Certainly," she said.

And *POOF!*

She sent them to Acapulco,

where they lived happily ever after,
between the devil and the deep blue sea.